I0566535

The Releasing of Shame

From dark secrets into His marvelous light

By D.L. Sullivan

ISBN: 0615601650

ISBN-13: 978-0-615-60165-6

Dedication

Thank you Holy Spirit for using me for such a time as this and for trusting me to reach your people.

To my awesome man of God; husband I love you dearly. I am privileged to be married to a man with such strong faith in order to establish God's purpose in the earth.

Denise Watson

Pastor Yuchong Seelye

Lewis Banks

&

All my family and friends

I love you

Contents

1

"9-1-1, what's your emergency?"

"It's my neighbor. She... she's hurt bad. There's blood... blood everywhere." In a stutter the voice stated.

"Okay ma'am, what's your name and what's wrong with your neighbor?" the police dispatcher asked in a stern voice.

"Ah, ah, my name is Susan, please hurry."

"Ok ma'am, I need you to try and stay calm for me so that we can help her. She's your neighbor correct?"

"Yes and best friend," Susan said breathing heavy.

"Susan what is your friend's address?" The dispatcher asked.

"Oh my God! Oh my God! I can't believe he did it," in a distraught voice Susan, uttered.

"Susan I need her address", the dispatcher repeated.

"It's 7...52 Warrensville Heights, ah apartment 7. He really went through with it," Susan babbling off in disbelief that reality set in.

"Susan what's your neighbor's name?" the dispatcher continued gathering her information.

"*Debra*, she stated."

"Okay where is Debra now Susan?"

"*Please I'm begging you; please hurry*," Susan said pleading desperately for help."

"Calm down Susan, so I can help you," the dispatcher replied trying to diffuse Susan's panic.

"*Okay*," in a childlike voice.

"Now, tell me where is Debra?"

"*She was lying on the sofa, when I left her apartment*," Susan's voice trembled.

"Okay ma'am, what happened?"

"I was watching TV when I heard this loud bang. It was so loud it scared me. Immediately after the noise I heard screaming. I opened my front door and the screaming sound like it was in the hallway, but I knew it was coming from down-stairs. I walked down-stairs to see what was going on. As I took each step down-stairs the screams grew louder and louder as if it was right in front of me." "When I reached the bottom of the stairs I could see Debra's door was open. It wasn't just opened, it was off the hinges. The door was completely kicked in. The door frame was broken and the wood looked shattered." Susan continued, "I couldn't believe my eyes." "I stood in the doorway. He had her pinned down to the sofa."

"Who had her pinned down?" The dispatcher questioned.

"*Patrick*."

Before the dispatcher could get another word in Susan continued.

"He had his right knee in her chest. Her legs were squirming."

"Susan what was he doing to her?" The dispatcher asked.

"*Something I*", Susan was beginning to cry.

"*Oh Lord what has he done?*"

"Susan, I need you to tell me what's wrong with your friend."

"He was beating her. I saw him punching Debra continuously. I told him to stop, but he wouldn't."

Susan blurted, "*Oh my GOD, If you don't hurry I don't know if she is going to make it.*"

The police dispatcher reassured her, "Susan I have paramedics on the way."

"*No, you don't understand.*" Susan stated in a mumbling voice.

"*I ran back upstairs to call you. I could still hear her screaming from the second floor. Now, I don't.*"

She began to cry.

"Susan listen to me, did he chase you?"

"No, but he looked right at me like he wanted to kill me, with death in his eyes, like he had a demon in him."

"What was he wearing?"

"Ahh, all black. *Please, please what's taking so long?*"

"The paramedics are not far Susan."

"How tall is he ma'am?"

"About 6 feet."

Police sirens were whistling. The police yelling in the background saying "check the perimeters." "Every apartment building will be searched, we will knock on doors if we have to, it may be a long day boys."

"Our Father who art in heaven, please don't let Debra die, not like this Lord, she has unfinished business here." Susan prayed while connected to 911.

"You're ok now", the dispatcher assured Susan.

"How do you know?" "Did you get a word from the Lord?"

"Well no," the operator replied; sorrowful she said something.

"I hear the paramedics and the police; they're there to help protect you."

Bang, Bang, Bang three knocks at the door.

"*Ahhhhh*," Susan screamed in fear.

"Susan look out your peep hole. Is it the police?"

Bang, bang, bang…"**POLICE OPEN UP**", the police yelled.

"Yes, it's the police."

"Okay you are going to be fine now. I'm going to hang up. Just open the door for the officers, they won't hurt you," the dispatcher commented in relief by their arrival.

"Okay."

"Goodbye Susan."

She opened the door right after hanging up.

"Ma'am is your name Susan?" an officer asked.

"Yes," Susan answered short and to the point.

"Susan, I'm Detective Wright and this is SGT. Howell, may we come in?"

Sadly Susan says, "Okay….come in."

Susan took a seat on her sofa. There was a bible on the coffee table that she picked up and held onto with both hands in her lap. Her legs trembled in fear. Detective Wright and SGT. Howell followed her into the living room; they both stood.

"We have the paramedics and officers at Debra's house now, but we really would like to get a statement from you. Would that be okay with you?" Detective Wright asked.

"I already told the police dispatcher. Is Debra going to be okay?" Susan said eager to know if Debra was alive or not.

"Ma'am we want to get a sworn statement so we can put whoever did this to your friend behind bars."

SGT. Howell informed Susan how important the statement was to the well-being of Debra.

"What do you mean whoever did it?" Susan questioned.

"Well there was no one at the crime scene when we got there, but officers are searching now," SGT Howell commented.

"I told the dispatcher that Patrick did it, I know you use radios," Susan blurted.

"We know you are tired and upset, but we really need your help right now."

Susan cried.

Visions of her friend's blood splattered on the walls and smeared on the sofa caused her to panic. The fear that Patrick instilled through his eyes compelled her to hold her bible like a child with a blanket.

"I heard noise and screaming. I opened my door; I could hear the screaming louder. When I got to Debra's house the door was open, but not by her. The door was completely off the hinges!"

"Ah, excuse me Susan," the detective interrupted her.

"I need you to tell me what you saw Patrick and Debra doing." The detective questioned.

Tears fell down her right cheek.

"Patrick had his right knee in her chest and his left leg was extended out on the floor. Debra's legs were moving. She was trying to get away. His back was to me but I believe he was punching her nonstop. Blood was on the walls and sofa. I told Patrick to stop, but he wouldn't. He turned and looked at me and it scared me. I thought he was going to beat me too."

"Did he say something to you or chase you?" Detective Wright wanted to know.

"No he didn't say anything or chase me, but his eyes were so cold like he was possessed," Susan's voice trembled.

Over SGT. Howell's radio another officer sound off saying, "We think we got our man, black, about 6 feet with all black on."

"We need you to come down to the station to identify our John Doe," Detective Wright informed Susan.

With anticipation Susan said, "You still haven't told me how Debra's doing?"

The officers glanced at each other. SGT. Howell's head dropped lower as he said, "We are sorry, but Debra was dead when we got here."

Susan looked up at Howell and smiled in denial of what she heard.

"Okay so what hospital did you take her to? I know she needs me right now, Susan asked not excepting Debra's death.

Detective Wright's phone rang. "Hello," he answered. "Okay I'll be right down." In an eager tone of voice he responded.

"Is everything alright?" SGT Howell asked the detective.

"Well I'm not sure. Are you going to be okay here with her?" "I really need to get down stairs to see what they came up with."

"Go, I'll be fine."

2

The body still warm, lying in a pool of blood on the couch; police covered her with a white sheet, feet exposed. The couch was a light color but barely noticeable because of the blood. The oversized teddy bear smothered in blood, glass on the floor from the picture frames that were once on Debra's coffee table.

"Hey Detective Wright, come take a look at this." Detective Smith shouted as soon as Detective Wright walked into her apartment.

Walking through the small two bedroom apartment trying to replay in his mind just what took place. In Debra's room Detective Smith was smiling while standing over Debra's queen size bed.

"What is it Smith?" Detective Wright asked.

"Come closer."

The bed had lots of pillows, far from neat, unmade as if Debra just stepped out the bed for a moment. There in the middle of the bed in between two pillows on her stomach, was a baby girl sleeping. She had all pink on, with tight dark curly hair, and a ball spot in the back.

"She slept through the whole murder." Detective Wright said.

"How she slept through all that noise, I don't know. I do know this is one blessed baby. Whoever killed her mother would have had no problem taking her out. This is one of the bloodiest cases I have been on. This guy had no conscious. She has another child too; a boy. The second bedroom has all his belongings in it." Detective Smith informed Detective Wright.

"Is he here too?" Detective Wright asked.

"No."

"Did you call DHR?"

"Yes, but family is on the way."

3

Twenty-four years ago on September the 5th, my birth certificate showed police that the baby girl was 21 months old and P.J. (Patrick Jr.); my brother was 10 years old. Rachel my first cousin on my father's side lived with us during this time. She was thirteen years old, but wasn't at home during the murder.

It's the Day after Christmas, my birthday and for the first time in 23 years I'm spending my birthday with Rachel and the Thomas family in Warrensville Heights, Ohio.

"How does that sound so far, Rachel?"

"Yes Kennedy that's true according to the trial. What are you up to?" Rachel asked.

"I'm writing a book. I've carried the shame of my past too long. It's time to help someone else. One morning the Lord spoke clearly to my heart.

"What did He say?" Rachel asked.

He said, "You're going to write a book. I no longer want you to live in the shame of your past."

"God wants me to share my testimony. I'm going to help women and men like me break free from the shame of their past with my story. I figured it's no better time to start than now, since dad is throwing me a birthday party."

"*Wow*, Kennedy that's great a lot of women need restoration, we go through so much and keep going like nothing ever happen, but we act out in other ways. I'm glad you could make it to Cleveland, especially during December with the snow and all."

"I'm glad you could make it Rachel. I know you work a lot."

"Baby I wouldn't have missed this for a job in the world. I can't believe it has been over twenty years since I helped your mom take care of you. You look just like her. We need to catch up. I want to know everything. I sure hate that you all moved down south, especially since PJ was here in Cleveland."

"Rachel you will get a better understanding of my life through my testimony, but I need your thoughts from the night of the murder for my book."

My life was personal to Rachel. Our mother was a mother figure to her. Everyone has that aunt in their life; the one they feel safe talking to. She kept in contact with me when we moved, but with a 13 year gap we never talked on a personal level. Rachel had part of mom back now.

"Twenty-four years and it still hurts that she's gone. I'll never forget the fear in Susan's eyes. She told the family...well the adults, I just ease dropped on what she saw that morning Rachel emphasized. It was unbelievable that my Uncle Patrick would stab Aunt Debra 31 times. It felt like a bad dream. I mean really, this dream lasted six ugly months. Me, you and PJ all ended up at Grandma Thomas's house. That was the hard part. Since Auntie Debra always came around the Thomas's, it was hard for Grandma Thomas to give you and PJ over to your granny. Which I felt was low down to an extinct since her son killed her daughter that was the least she could have did. But no, it went to trial. The death was hard on me because you became clingy to me and I was only a child myself. I was babysitter turned mommy now. All you would do was cry if I wasn't in your presence. When I come home from school Grandma Thomas would say, *"Get ya baby."* People at school thought I had a baby. I had no privacy from you. When I'd use the bathroom, I couldn't lock the door or you would lie down on your back kicking the bathroom door, screaming at the top of your lungs, "**LET ME IN**." It messed me up. So I started smoking cigarettes, but you told on me while I was at school by taking crayons and using them as cigarettes. I'm really proud of you and how you turned out. You know the family really wanted to meet your husband; maybe he can make it next time. Please tell more about your life."

"Ok let me finish chapter one."

Sleeping through what papers called the slaying of Debra, was just a pivot point in my life.

4

"*Noo,*" I cried for Uncle Kevin; my father's baby brother.

"It's okay Kennedy, it's going to be okay," he tried to reassure me with tears in his eyes.

As Granny picked me up from Grandma Thomas's home, I knew PJ and I wouldn't be together anymore. The grandparents battled in court for us both, but the courts decided to separate us between the two families. So I went with Granny and Papa, our mother's parents and PJ stayed with Grandma Thomas.

No one seen what was coming just five years later, Granny and Papa, moved from Ohio to Alabama, Papa's home town. I have no clue how anyone could work at one place for 40 years but Papa did it. He was a plant worker until it closed. They gave Papa his pension and he never worked again. Now over 700 miles separated me from my brother and my mommy-cousin, Rachel.

I adjusted to Alabama rather quickly.

Three years later. At ten years old with granny and papa pushing sixty and a 50 year age gap; life was not exciting unless I made my own.

"Papa, can I go outside and play with Sarah?" I anxiously asked.

"Go ask your grandmother." Papa responded.

Yes Granny ran the show in our house. They were extremely strict and afraid that everyone wanted to kidnap me. The news these days can really instill fear in parents.

Sarah was my friend and our neighbor. We played together every day after school. We lived in the suburbs thirty minutes outside of Birmingham, Alabama. Granny made sure I went to the best schools, so we lived in the best neighborhoods. The bible says that God is no respecter of persons, but I learned neither is the devil. The enemy doesn't care about your address or what neighborhood it's in, what kind of car you drive, or how old you are. I learned he plots his attacks early in life, trying to build a breaking point. I never knew my mother but I'm thankful she was saved, and fought the good fight of faith because God's blessings are generational. On the flip side the devil's curses can be generational as well.

Sarah was white with beautiful blonde thin hair, naturally straight, bangs, round dark brown eyes, thin but fully developed at ten years old. I was the complete opposite; skinny, black, with thick long dark brown hair, that reached the middle of my back with green eyes.

"Granny, I asked papa if I can go outside and play with Sarah and he said to ask you if I could go outside."

"Yes, but you better have your little narrow tail in here before it gets dark, don't make me come looking for you."

There were no loving words in our home, if so it was sarcastic, and everything was negative or a joke, that's their way of expressing themselves. My grandparents loved me the only way they knew how, but neither knew how to show love, not even to each other. I only saw them kiss in front of me once. I never seen them hold hands or speak words of affirmation to one another. If I didn't say I loved them....I wouldn't-of heard it.

Longing for the family I didn't get a chance to know, not that it would-of been any better. Often wondering how my mother was, what she would sound like, or if she was funny or a serious person. Granny only had one adult picture of her and no movies with her on it. More than anything, I yearned for love in action.

Sarah and I rode bicycles up and down the street as fast as we could back and forth. Papa would come out to keep an eye on me and walk across the street to his friend Archie's house. They could talk for hours in his garage, both retired and in their late 50's.

Mr. Archie was white with thin, dark brown hair, so thin you could see his scalp through his neatly combed hair, teeth were stained from cigarettes, coffee and old age. He stood about 6 feet tall, slim but walked with a limp and a cane at times. Archie was married with grandchildren. His wife unlike him was not retired.

Summer came in Alabama. It was only three things to do for kids our age...go to the movies, skating, or swimming. But with the grandparents paranoia I was unable to do anything...almost.

"Granny can I get dropped off at the movies." I asked.

"No! Have you lost your mind? What you think, you grown or something? Don't you know its people out here snatching little kids every day?" Granny enlightened me.

Granny was a pretty woman who kept her hair cut short and dyed between a honey blonde and a light brown, naturally wavy; she stood 5 feet 3 inches with brown eyes and thin lips, with a full figure.

"Papa, please let me go to the movies."

"Didn't she tell you no." he said in a loud deep voice.

Papa stood about 6 feet tall, dark brown skinned, medium build, with a full grey mustache, and grey hair around the sides of his head only.

The only thing left to do was swim that summer, but not really because I couldn't swim.

"These old folks make me sick, I can't do nothing," mumbling under my breath.

"What you say?" Granny asked.

"Oh nothing Granny."

"I thought you was talking back...you better sit yo fast tail down somewhere." She warned me.

"Okay." I said.

I needed something to do with my time. I asked about camp.

Granny said, "summer camp is not an option. We are on a fixed income Kennedy."

Alabama got hot in the summers. Riding bikes was not exciting in 100 degree weather. There had to be something to do, to keep cool.

"Granny can I go play in the sprinklers with Sarah?" I pleaded.

"Okay, be where I can see you." She said.

Thankfully I said, "Thank you Granny."

What a blast running through the sprinklers. I could see Papa walking to Mr. Archie's house. Now he owned his own in ground swimming pool, but I couldn't swim so what was the use in asking. I'm sure Granny would be concerned about me drowning.

"Your granddaughter and her friend can use my swimming pool as long as I'm home." He told Papa.

"Kennedy!" Papa yelled from across the street.

"Yes Papa!" I yelled back.

I continued to run through the sprinklers trying to listen at the same time.

"*Come here.*" Papa demanded.

Running across the street with no shoes on, the ground was hot so I ran rather fast.

"Yes Papa," I asked.

"Do you and Sarah wanna go swimming? Mr. Archie has been nice enough to invite y'all to use his pool."

"Oh Papa I would love to."

"Thank you Mr. Archie!"

"Any time," he said.

Papa said, "Make sure Sarah asks her mother."

"Ok Papa."

Running back across the street smiling, I could hardly wait to tell Sarah.

"Sarah...Sarah" I screamed.

"Papa said, ask your mom if you can go swimming. Mr. Archie said we can use his pool.

"My mom's not at home. She had to work, but I will ask my sister Beth to call her at work."

It wasn't ten minutes later when Sarah and her younger brother Parker was ready to have some fun. Parker was only a year younger than us, making him nine at the time.

Sarah said, "My sister made me bring him so she wouldn't have to put up with him. My mother is taking Parker to our grandmother's house for the summer so an adult can watch after him because he's so active; but we can go swimming."

I don't think it rained the entire summer in Alabama. There was no relief from the heat unless you stayed inside, went swimming, or it was December....long summers and short winters.

"Do you know how to swim?" I asked Sarah.

"Yeah," She answered.

"Oh," I said.

We were only ten, so I was wondering how old was she when she started swimming, *five*. I knew adults who couldn't swim, so I was amazed.

Sarah laughed and said, "What you wanna go swimming, but you can't swim?"

I use to be afraid of water, but I wasn't gonna tell her that.

"Well Papa just hasn't shown me yet."

After sitting on the steps on the shallow end watching Sarah and Parker do cannon balls off the diving board into the deep end, and all I could do was use the goggles to look under water. Without them my eyes would burn. I was determined to learn. I begged Papa to take me to get lessons. Papa enjoyed sports, especially golf. So it wouldn't be hard getting him to take me. Finally, Papa gave in when he found out that one of the local pools was having free swimming lessons. I learned in two weeks. Papa bought me some purple goggles to match my one piece bathing suit. It was purple on the front and black on the back. I skipped a couple of steps in the lessons since I wasn't afraid of water anymore. I was thrilled not to be around the other kids who were afraid of water. They would practically drown you with their doggy peddling while splashing water into my goggles causing them to fog. Every day for two weeks straight Papa took me until my swimming coach Ms. Carol, told Papa I was finished with my lessons. Soon as I learned Papa let me go to Mr. Archie's house with Sarah by myself because he was a TV lover. You would think after swimming every day, we *would-of* been tired, but we never were.

5

It was almost July, around twelve noon lunch time, but Mr. Archie's wife never came home for lunch, I noticed.

Mr. Archie asked Sarah and me, *"Do y'all girls want some lunch?"*

"Yes sir," we said with enthusiasm.

Sarah and I didn't like to walk home knowing we wanted to get back in the pool. Mr. Archie's home was two stories. Walking in from the backyard led directly into the kitchen eating area. The walls in the kitchen were white with blue wallpaper boarder going around between the cabinets and the counters. The cabinets were dark but the counter tops were off white. It was an eat-in kitchen in which they had a long oak wood table in the kitchen that seated six people at a time; two in the middle on opposite sides and one on each end of the table. Next to it was the family den; vaulted ceiling which made the room seem much bigger than it actually was. The house was filled with natural light, but the brown carpet made it appear dim.

I still remember the cloth brown sectional sofa. The TV was around 27 inches inside an oak cabinet that had glass doors on top, with oak cabinet drawers below, two drawers on opposite sides had custom locks. I believe he bought the cabinet that way. That day for lunch we had ham sandwiches, chips with a soda.

Mr. Archie sat down in his regular spot…I noticed by the wrinkle butt imprint on the sofa that faced directly in front of the TV. Where Sarah was sitting she could see the TV, I couldn't. She was at the end of the table. I was sitting on the side of the table.

"Do y'all want to see a movie?" he asked.

We said, "yes sir!" excitedly.

Fumbling through his keys he finds the short gold key, the smallest key on the key ring and opens the drawer on the oak cabinet. He takes out the VHS tape with no writing on it. Before putting it into the VCR, he says, "If y'all can keep a secret I will show y'all."

I couldn't hold water, but of course we both said, "We can keep a secret."

He looked at me and said, "Now you can't tell your Papa, or he won't let you go swimming anymore."

"Okay I won't tell him."

This must be a really good movie, I'm sure Papa wouldn't mind watching it. He loves movies and sports. Swimming became my passion and I couldn't let anything mess that up. Soon as he put the movie in it wasn't wound up and immediately I heard moaning noises. It was a lady and man having sex. Pornography! I knew I couldn't tell Papa or Granny. They didn't have sex nor kiss or hold hands for all I was aware of.

While Papa watched TV his friend was awakening my sexuality. This was foreign to me and Sarah; we'd never seen a grown naked man's body. Shame quickly came over me because they were naked. It was a lot to process at that age. Sarah and I continued going over Mr. Archie's house that summer. Consumed with lust, he exposed us to the spirit of perversion while showing us Playboy Magazines and same sex pornography. All the extra attention and time we spent with Mr. Archie, felt like love and I was longing for love. This felt close enough. He was nice to us and told us we were pretty, never sarcastic or negative.

6

Rachel in disbelief moved from side to side in her seat and her eyes began to swell with water.

"Listen I can stop, if you'd like?"

"No keep reading, it just reminded me of something."

He would look at our bodies and ask us to touch each other like the women in the videos. Both of us still in damp bathing suits, he would ask us to either take off the straps of the top of our bathing suits or slide over the bottom portion to view our private areas. We followed his directions and slid our straps. That wasn't good enough for him.

He said, *"Naw wait. Do it like the girls in the video.*

We hesitated.

"Come on yawl do it for me. Trust me your gonna like it. Go head!"

We wanted to please this man; after all he'd been so nice to us. At night lustful sensations grew in my body that I wasn't use to having, they felt good. Never hearing about lust, I can remember being a slave to pornography. Like a drug addict just waiting for the next hit. Granny would be in bed by 9 o'clock faithfully every night, but she wouldn't fall asleep until after the 10 o'clock news would go off. By that time Papa showered and got in bed. When his head hit the pillow, he was sleep. Granny on the other hand was a light sleeper and I would have to sit around until I could hear her snoring.

Now in our house we didn't have the playboy channel, but we did have HBO. By the time Granny went to sleep all the late night pornography was off. My nightly routine was to turn to the playboy channel that we didn't have and between the fuzzy lines I'd watched the people have sex. I learned self-pleasing at an early age by watching these movies in which I was a slave to as well, 2 Peter 2:14 "Sin is never satisfied."

In the 5th grade and addicted to masturbation, I couldn't get through school without going to the bathroom lining the bathroom seat so I could get another hit.

Rachel could no longer hold back her tears.

"Kennedy did you tell your grandparents?"

"No."

"Why-not?"

With tears in my eyes, I could feel fear trying to rise. Fear didn't want me to release the shame of my past; things I never shared with anyone. Until I heard GOD's still small voice say, "You are free. I don't want you bound to shame. Tell her how I brought you out of darkness."

"They were already afraid everyone wanted to hurt me; that would-of made it worse for me because I couldn't do anything as it was. I enjoyed being around him because he made me feel good about being me. I liked the feeling of lust. So I felt like it was my fault. We moved shortly after to a nicer suburb with better schools. Since we moved, I blocked Mr. Archie and the whole situation out. It's amazing how you can trick your mind to forget your past. But I tell you what, the Holy Spirit doesn't forget. He will minister to your inner man. He saved me."

Smiling, nose still red from crying Rachel said, "Girl you remind me so much of your mother after she got saved."

"How was she?" I was eager to know more of her.

Family always gave vague details of mom.

"I don't know, she just loved God, wasn't one of those closet freaks. Who love God only on Sunday and cuss you out on Monday. She was just different. You know I'm not churchy so you asking the wrong person."

"If he did it for me, he can do it for you. You know the bible says in Acts 10:34, God is no respecter of person."

Rachel listened, but wanted to know more of my life.

"So when you all moved away, were you still into the movies?" Rachel curiously asked.

"You mean pornography."

I had to speak the word pornography because for so long I couldn't voice it. The shame had me mute.

"Yes pornography," Rachel said.

It was great to see Rachel speak the word without shame. She began to dig deeper, she asked, "And that didn't remind you of the neighbor?"

"No, it didn't. It made me feel better. I didn't think much of myself and neither did Granny and Papa. Once I shared a dream with Granny that I was going to be a designer when I grew up. Do you know what she told me?"

"What?" Rachel asked.

"Aw girl don't you know you black? Black and broke, two things against you. You won't make it being no designer. I wouldn't waist money sending you to school for something you'd never get a job doing."

I needed something or maybe someone to make me feel better.

7

"Paper or plastic," I asked every customer that came through my line.

"Did you like working?" Rachel asked.

"No, I worked about thirty-three hours a week and I only made around one hundred-fifty dollars a week after taxes. I had to work or be without. The friction in our home between Granny and me became intense. The negativity was unbearable. I would come home and not speak, eat, stay in my room and do it all over again the next day. Granny resented me not wanting to be around her and would seek revenge."

She would say to people while in my presence, *"That's ok that heifer will need me before I need her."*

The winter before I got the job, I remember needing a coat.

I said, "Granny I need a coat."

She said, *"Kennedy, I-DON'T- HAVE- NO- MONEY."*

I walked back to my room in tears, not that she didn't have the money, but that she did have the money and would be so evil. The next day my best friend gave me her black old, leather coat and I was grateful. By the end of the week, I'll never forget it; Granny went to Macy's and bought herself an eighty dollar, black leather coat and had the nerve to show it off to me.

She said, "Look, I caught a sale."

It hit me. If she could watch me walk around in the cold with no coat and have the money; I needed a job fast.

At only fourteen years old with a workers permit; I had my very first job. My first year in high school with c's and d's in every class except introductory computer, physical education, and eating lunch. I had an 'A' in all three. I believed the lie that I was dumb, so I never tried. Scholarships were not in my near future.

School wasn't much better than home, far as rejection. Thanks to TJ Maxx and Marshalls, I bought name brand clothes as low as $5.99. I had four girls that I called friends. The rest were associates and the others were haters; and there were many others. To let girls tell it I thought I was all that. The truth was they thought I was all that. I had thoughts of myself but *all of that* was not one of them. The girls at school didn't want to know me, too afraid I would take their boyfriends. Fights broke out over the smallest things and I was suspended so many times that the principal told my grandparents one more time and we will have to send her to alternative school.

Resentment set in. I was beginning to become hard. Feelings of anger and lust still consumed me. In hopes of getting love at 15 years old, I decided to have sex. If there was any whole pieces left to my heart, this completely shattered whatever was left.

I never told about Mr. Archie, but the loss of my virginity left me broken. It coerced me to tell Granny. She was angry at me; as if we talked sex before and been taught better.

"If you pregnant, you and that baby getting out my house; I raised my brothers, my own kids and now YOU and I aint raising no-mo kids."

"I'm not pregnant," I yelled back at her.

"Well you bet-not have sex again. When you get married your husband won't know the difference."

"What you mean Granny?"

"If you don't have sex again your body will go back to normal and your husband won't know the difference."

I couldn't believe Granny said that. I wonder did she tell Papa something similar since he was my Step-Papa; maybe she told him she only been with her first husband. I call these shameful lies; *flesh satisfiers*. It was obvious I had no safe place to turn. Granny was teaching me to deceive my husband at fifteen. I was broken and need fixing.

Rachel looked at me as if she could feel the painful experience herself.

She murmured, "Not being excepted for any reason must have been hard."

Hard was belittlement. Bored and lonely, I didn't bury myself in the television, I resented TV. TV was my grandparent's lives while I hungered and thirst for love. At one point we had TVs in every room; a 13 inch in the kitchen, in the den a broke floor monitor TV and one that worked sitting on top of it. No one asked how my days were. TV was fuel to the fire. I already knew how their days were, filled with talk shows and negative news reports.

Whenever I wasn't working or at school, morning or night, my bedroom was my dark cave. Yep, I was a bear in hibernation. I hibernated in the cave for four years. Outside was cold. So, I locked myself in there.

"The cave was chaotic. My life was loud. Turning up the stereo as loud as possible help drown out my life around me. Rap was my favorite. I started believing in the lyrics about women being easy, especially whenever I finally turned on the TV to MTV or BET, only to watch rap videos. The women would just smile as the rappers would pour champagne over their heads and they would smile like it was fun. Rap music started raising me. The painful hurt and self-pity quickly turned into anger…resentment, and my actions turned foolish.

With time to dream, big dreams, my grade point average was closer to 1.0 than 4.0. I wanted to be a rapper. I learned to cuss and I was really good at it. Writing rhymes passed the time; some of the guys at school I grew up with wanted to be rappers too. I would try to free style, but I was terrible at it. Writing was my release, not just rhymes, but poetry and I didn't forget to write letters to God.

Yes, in the midst of my foolishness, I found time to talk to God. My girlfriend's mom told me to write my prayers down that my prayers would come to pass quicker.

In tears while writing to God; God will you let my mother come visit me? I wondered would she ever show. I waited for her. Patiently expecting her to show up in a dream or come visit. Mad at her for the stories I always heard from family that she would allow dad to treat her wrong for years. Granny said they use to fight in high school. Who would have kids by an idiot? I wondered.

Resenting her decisions caused me to question God.

Praying to God I said, "you let us be motherless and fatherless. Enraged at God, why us? Why didn't you keep

me and PJ together? At least we could have had each other.
Granny and Papa love me in their weird way. You and I both
know God, that no one can love me like my own mom."

Granny always said I was old for my age. Speaking to God
on a regular basis in the cave, I broke it down to Him why I
was so mad I didn't have my own mom.

God when you allow a mother to be pregnant with a child for
nine months, there's a bonding stage. You give them an
umbilical cord, the mother feeds her child, but the child also
feeds the mother; it changes her taste buds and her moods
even the way she sees life. The final stage after nursing the
child to life, she gives birth, but she has to release the
placenta, it's the after birth. The placenta is what protects
that baby. Convinced granny couldn't love me because I
wasn't her birth child. God in that placenta is love,
encouragement, and protection, I'm sure of it."

Often wondering why me God? Why me?

"What did God tell you?" Rachel asked.

"It wasn't until after high school it came to my
realization; prayer is a two-way conversation. I thought God
only listened."

"What does he sound like now?"

"Well the best way to describe Him is, He gives me a
thought. The scripture that gave me the best understanding
to God's voice is Isaiah 55:8, "for my thoughts are not your
thoughts, neither are your ways my ways saith, the LORD."

My bible collected dust while in high school. I only cleaned
and dusted my bible off on Sundays. Reading the word of
God was too much like school work. The King James
Version felt like Algebra 2, *trying to figure out the*

equations. Well I received an 'f' in Algebra 2. It was the only class I had to go to summer school for. Other times reading the King James Version felt like Spanish Class, completely foreign. We only went to church on Sunday's; I thought bible study was for the preachers kids. We'd be all dressed up on the outside with no word on the inside. Granny with her fine suits and expensive panty hose from JCPenney's. She was a missionary and they wore all white on certain Sunday's. I didn't even know missionaries went on missions.

High school graduation was exciting. It was the only thing I'd ever completed. The church gave me the New International Version as a graduation gift. *Man, I really could-of used that in school.* If I read my word, at least I'd known God's people perish for a lack of knowledge, Hosea 4:6.

Well since I graduated with a 1.0 grade point average or something close to it, college was not in my plans. Just two months later I was saying I do to Uncle Sam and yes to the United States Navy.

8

"*Heeyy Thomas*," Emilio screamed across the pier.

Enforcing my point I said, "Emilio what have I told you about calling me by my government name when were not at work? I don't want everyone knowing my name."

My last name was my first name to Uncle Sam. I never liked being called by that name not just because it connected me to my father, but it seemed like prison, just another number, you know…no identity.

"*You know I'm sorry boo, but I be forgetting Uncle Sam got me all messed up*," he implied.

Oh great, I thought to myself. Emilio didn't get smart with me. What does he want? You see he was Puerto Rican and black, there was no getting an attitude with him and get away with it.

He was handsome light skinned, six feet tall, straight jet black hair, but often used gel to spike it, with thick jet black eyebrows that were neatly trimmed. Emilio also had a great personality. There was something different about him; I couldn't quite put my finger on.

We bonded. The closer we got he told me his secret, he was gay. This did not affect our friendship, though I didn't agree with the lifestyle. Maybe he'd been hurt like me.

Females were crazy over Mr. Rodriguez.

Getting off work, walking down the pier the females would pass by saying, *"Hey Rodriguez."*

"Hey," he said back.

With his arm around my neck we would laugh. Both of us new to the military and only eight-teen, I was four days older than him.

Emilio finally asked me, "Do you want to get a contract?"

"What kind of contract? You know leadership said to be careful."

During in-processing class, leadership informed the new sailors what to look out for. Like buying cars and various items; to first have legal review it.

"Girl, I'm talking about a marriage contract. I'm tired of living on the ship, I need my own spot. Everyone is doing it; we can split the money and be roommates," He said trying to sell his contract like a true salesman."

"Everyone is doing what, getting fake married?"

Naïve, very much so, I might have been a dummy my whole life *but crazy was pushing it.* I couldn't get married to a gay man. I loved Emilio, but I wasn't in love with him.

Tickled...laughing Rachel asked, "So what did you do?"

I told him, "Rodriguez, I really want to get off the ship too, but if it takes marrying you I better learn to swim. Are you crazy? I continued chastising him like Granny did me growing up. What if you decide you don't want to be gay anymore and really want to get married? Shoot, the love of my life may ask me to get married; what would I tell him? Well ah, I can't because I'm married to my gay friend."

"Okay, okay...I get it. You don't want to get married, but don't be trying to come to my house and stay when I move."

"Please, I don't need to stay with you."

A month later Emilio got married to some woman that needed health insurance and that was all she wanted from him.

We were stationed on 32nd street in San Diego, California. It felt like I was in another country compared to Alabama. I didn't know there was a thing as gay communities. Driving into Hill Crest, I parked my brand new car...well brand new to me. In California, you can't mess around, they still have gangs and they steal cars; I was just a bit worried. I parked in front of the address Emilio gave me and called him on my cell.

"Emilio, come down; I'm outside," I demanded.

He came out with his white, wife beater, and Armani Jeans on.

I rolled the window down and said, "Hey is my car going to be safe here?"

He laughed and said, *"Girl the only thing they gone steal around here...is yo-man; come on in."*

He walked me into the apartment. It was neatly decorated. Not like a bachelor pad, but almost as if a woman lived there. In the bathroom Emilio had hair products and make-up all over the bathroom counter.

As he finished getting dressed while looking at himself in the mirror he asked, *"Is that what you're wearing out to eat?"*

I used the toilet seat in the bathroom as a chair while he got ready. I looked down at my outfit; I had on shorts, a t-shirt and sandals. My feet were always done professionally, but I didn't wear make-up, just lip gloss from MAC.

"I look good, I don't know what you talking about. I didn't know you wore make-up?" I questioned him.

"Yes boo...just concealer and foundation. I stay flawless and you should too. You should consider getting your eyebrows waxed. You're a pretty girl but you should go the extra mile, to be the best looking girl. Now I see why you don't have a man." He said, in a serious-nonchalant tone of voice.

"Yeah, you stole him from me." I laughed.

That was our friendship open, except our past. Both bound to the shameful demons, both trying to rationalize our foolish behavior. My lust and his perversion were our masters. It makes people feel uncomfortable including the person shackled to the sin.

I looked up at Emilio as he put his concealer and foundation on. I had compassion towards him; as he covered his inner loneliness and sin with make-up, mine was covered in sheets and blankets in the middle of my bed with the darkness that night time brought.

I asked him, "What happened to you, to not like girls?"

Looking at him was looking into a mirror.

No, I wasn't lesbian. The thoughts would cross my mind. Remembering how Sarah and I would touch each other to please the neighbor. Mr. Archie planted seeds in me and one was the spirit of perversion. As an adult I never entertained this spirit.

Not knowing to some extinct I feared God and was applying 2 Corinthians 10:5 "Take every thought and make it obedient to Christ." If so I could have applied the same principal to self-pleasing and pornography.

At this stage in my life I didn't consider myself a backslider. In my mind I was saved. I talked to God and he listened. It was normal to me if you went to church on Sunday you were saved. I knew people who partied Friday and Saturday, drank liquor, cuss you out, and play the number after they leave the sanctuary on Sunday.

Emilio was shocked by my question.

He said, "We had an uncle that use to mess with me and my brother. I don't remember it that well, but my brother told me. I can't remember everything, but I've been gay along time.

Listening to him tell his story, I knew he didn't want to remember. The shame creates denial. Over the years I, myself forgot a lot of my own past.

He said, "There was a chick I was close to who tried to see if I liked women. She pulled down her underwear to show me and I threw-up."

He had a sour look on his face remembering what she'd showed him.

Grievous to him, I didn't continue to question his past. We would talk about what we wanted to be when we grew up. It's easy to dream when you hate the life you live. He drove a Chrysler 300, the new body that resembled a Bentley.

Emilio asked me, *"Doesn't this car just make you feel rich?"*

I laughed and said, "Yes, Emilio."

When we got paid we treated ourselves to some of the finest restaurants. The best part of Emilio was his child-like character to dream. While eating filet mignon and sipping fine wine, our interest in the future grew intense.

"So, this Navy thing is not going to work for me; I don't know about you but I'm going places. I won't look this good forever. I need to get to L.A. and try to start my career," Emilio went on about his dreams.

Trying to be more realistic than my cave dreams of being a rapper, I decided I wanted to own a business.

"After the Navy, I hope I never have to work for anyone again. I would like to be a business woman and own a night club."

I figured I could offer people secular music calling women out their names and sell liquor and still be saved...right? Wrong again.

"Well you can catch me on the cover of a magazine; I'm definitely going to be a model," he emphasized.

I had dreams of being many things...from fashion designer to a rapper, even considered being what Granny acknowledged, being a nurse. I had to find my way. I chose the Navy to help find that way.

As time went on Emilio was trying to find his way and so was I. Our paths took us in different directions, still friends just different journeys. Emilio every opportunity that came up, would be in Los Angeles. I still hung around 32nd street in San Diego, doing my research about business.

9

The career counselor, a Senior Chief in the Navy asked me what I wanted to do.

I told her, "Well Senior, I want to be a Hospital Corpsman and I would like to someday own my own night club."

She smiled at me and handed me a pre-requisite sheet for the Navy job description and on-the-job training hourly sheet.

"Make sure your ASVAB scores are high enough for the job you want. Good luck, and by the way Chief Douglas owns his own club let me introduce you to him."

Senior walked me to Chief Douglas's desk.

"Hey Chief," Senior Chief said, "This is Seaman Thomas. This is her first duty station and she has a few goals she is trying to accomplish including owning her own night club someday. I was telling her about your night club; maybe you can give her your point of view from the business prospective."

"Sure no problem, thanks a lot Senior. I see you trying to get me some competition, joking sarcastically," Chief Douglas stated.

Chief Douglas was black. Dark skinned kept a low haircut, with a medium build about 6'0 feet tall and saturated in cologne daily.

"What's up Thomas? So you want to own your own night club. It's a lot of work and a huge liability. From insurance in case someone gets hurt or worse killed, to making sure people are not stealing from you on the inside...you know the employees."

I knew it would take hard work but the freedom it would provide for me was the lifestyle, I desired. My life was always what was best for me and me only. Since all I had was me.

"How old are you Thomas?" he asked.

"I'm 18. In two months I will be 19."

It went from trying to figure out the business to being under aged drinking and sleeping with this married man. I only drank when I was going to the club, I never did like the taste of alcohol but I liked how loose it made me feel.

A product of my environment where no one cared about marriage; most were fake anyway, I was conformed to worldly things. It only took a little alcohol to water that adulterous seed that was planted at ten. I was the other woman before I lost my virginity.

Meeting every prerequisite for the job, I left San Diego and never looked back. I didn't have to, I left with baggage. I went to two schools in one year maintaining an 'A-B' average in both. Shocked at my performance since I'd partied through both; only difference, I applied myself.

The club scene was getting old. At 21, when it was actually legal to drink alcohol; I was tired of that life. Partying in foreign countries with the Navy, I wanted more to life. I didn't know how to get more from life. Luckily in the Navy we moved a lot, maybe I could start over.

10

Destiny calls…the Navy called it duty or a duty station, but this time even farther from home. With military orders to Hawaii, I could start over. I tried to push the reset button on my life. There was something different about this location other than the island being beautiful and the cost of living more expensive; I was looking for something.

My cell phone rang. "Hello," I answered.

"Lil-sis, what's up?" PJ asked.

PJ and I faithfully went 10 months without talking. Ten months is the length between February and December. PJ's birthday is in February and mine in December; we'd only call on those days, not even Christmas some years. It was only January; I was concerned to be hearing from him.

"Hey PJ, How are you? Are you okay? Did something happen?"

PJ laughs. "No, I'm good…I'm good, and you?"

"Well I recently moved to Hawaii."

PJ said, "Man I need to visit."

PJ always said he was going to visit and never showed. He did make it to my High School graduation; I never knew when he was serious.

"Listen lil-sis I need to ask you a question."

I knew it was something to this call.

"Your father called me from prison. He said he getting out next week and he wanna talk to you."

"My father, that's yo father too. I thought he had 15 years to life."

"Yeah well he did 17 and I guess the state tired of paying for'em or sum'em."

"How did he get your number?"

"Look man, do you want me to give'em yo number or not?"

"Yeah you can give'em my number."

"Alright gotta go."

We hung up. I knew PJ was feeling some kind of way, but I wasn't sure which way.

I wasn't looking for him. Thinking to myself, what on earth do we have to talk about? Two weeks past I didn't hear anything from him. I'd wondered if PJ gave him my phone number.

11

Since fifteen, God has given me vivid dreams, but I never dreamed of my mom. Four years I waited for Debra, to show up in the cave. In the middle of the ocean, I will never forget what she said to me in my dream.

With tears in Rachel's eyes she asked, "What did she say?"

"I just got to Hawaii, living in the barracks when I dreamed of her. In the dream the phone was ringing; I was calling her. My father answered the phone…Hello? I said to him, let me talk to Debra. I asked for her by her first name and I don't know how I knew that was his or her voice. He told me she was tired, I demanded he put her on the phone."

She answered excitingly. The only thing she said was *"hey baby I am so proud of you."*

"Mom I really need to ask you something."

She said, *"Baby, I'm tired…mommies tired, I have to go now."* The dream ended before I could ask her the question.

Though I don't remember her at 21 months, I absolutely know that was her and her tone of voice when she was living. I can't explain it.

Rachel said, "Do you think that's what you were looking for?"

"It was great hearing from her. My heart melted knowing that my mother, the lady who birthed me was proud of me. I wasn't proud of me, but she was.

What could she possibly be proud of?

Ready to change, I read Self-help book after self-help book from *Never Be Lied To Again, How to Get What You Want Out of Life* to *How to Get A Man To Do What You Want.* I started buying the audio books so I could listen in the car. Borders was my favorite bookstore; they always had a sale.

"Hello Kennedy," the employees at the bookstore greeted me walking through the door.

The book store was home away from home; when problems arose I ran home.

"These books were knowledgeable but couldn't fill the void I was looking for."

On the other hand I was a people pleaser. The fear of being alone was greater than finding this void. Often forced to be alone, I longed for fellowship.

Life has a funny way of testing us. It will make sure you've had enough of your own foolishness. I didn't care for clubs. I once fell asleep in one. I said I'd never go back after that. Well I lied. The company I kept liked to party. Shortly after starting my new job I met Sean, my boyfriend who worked with me.

He was hilarious and a great friend but we never should have been lovers. He was married, but separated. His divorce went through shortly after, but that didn't make it ok.

Clinging to him, subconsciously hoping he doesn't leave like my mother did. In the cave wanting her, knowing I couldn't have her. The loneliness consumed me in the lowliness of the cave, but I had him now. I held on tight to something that was never mine.

The relationship was far from healthy. He would break up with me for looking wrong. Heartbreaking, too much like childhood; I couldn't get anything right.

My self-help got me nowhere. I was invited to church during one of our break ups. I will never forget this church, Word of Life. The people were genuine and friendly, man **they loved God**. The worship was authentic, I could tell even the congregation worshipped at home on a daily basis. The youth was on fire and unashamed of the gospel.

That evening after church my phone rang. "Hello," I answered.

There was no response. I glanced at my cell to see the number; I noticed it was a Cleveland area code and whoever it is, was still on the line.

"HELLO," I said again, but louder.

"Yes is this Kennedy?" He asked.

It was the same voice from my dream.

"Yes it is," I said.

"Hi this is Patrick, your father. I got out of prison three weeks ago. I don't know where to start but I know I need to start somewhere. I'm sorry baby. Will you forgive me?"

"I've already forgiven you, but why did you do it?"

He began to cry loudly. This was kind of awkward because I began to feel sympathy towards him.

His voice shook in a regretful stutter, "I..I..I wa-wa-was full of cocaine and alcohol that night. I was jealous of her new boyfriend and I couldn't handle her keeping you away from me. For years we fought saying we would kill each other, but neither one of us meant it. I took the knife over there that night to scare her, but I was so high, I went through with it. While stabbing her, I was out of it. It felt like I was poking her with a pin. And before I knew it, she was lying on the couch in a pool of blood."

"Because of you, I grew up not knowing who I looked like or sound like, without my big brother, or what it felt like to have a sibling, or to say the word mom or to see her smile or what made her sad. I could only live life through other people's memories of her and see her in the reflection of their eyes, but...I forgive you."

Still crying he said, "I'm truly sorry. Thank you for your forgiveness. Can I call you more?"

"I have a lot going on in my life right now, but yes we will talk more. I have to go now."

"Okay baby, talk to you soon."

We hung up. I cried. It was a lot going on in one day. I'm glad I went to church today. I received the word, but the word was choked by the weeds in my life.

Shortly after, Sean and I got back together. I asked him if he believed in God. He told me no. We were in bad shape because he was the first person I'd ever met that didn't. The bible says even demons believe there's a God. I wasn't any better than him; I believed in God, but I didn't fear Him. I didn't know God. I never read his word; I chose self- help books over his word. I was tired, tired of accepting less in every aspect of life. Remembering the joy and love I felt at that church, I wanted what they had. I'd been looking for

God's love in all the wrong places. Finally ready to crack open my bible, I went to the book store and walked right past the self-help aisle with my head held high. I needed Jesus; straight to the religion aisle I went.

A week later I decided I wanted to have a relationship with dad. I picked up the phone and call the number he called me from.

The phone rang.

He answered, "*Hi baby.*"

It seemed weird hearing him call me baby at first. I wasn't use to it. I never heard affectionate words like that growing up.

"Uh hi," I said back.

"I'm glad you called me back."

"I want to have a relationship with you. You and PJ is all I have for immediate family."

I could hear him crying, but trying not to make too much noise.

"I would like to hear more stories about my mom."

"Okay baby I have plenty of stories. Now I need to know something before we start. Can I be completely open and honest with you? Or do I have to sugar coat things and leave certain parts out?"

I was amazed. That's exactly what I needed, his honesty. And that's how he's been consistently for seven years and I appreciate it.

"I wouldn't have it any other way," I said. "First I would like to know about Susan. Granny told me you harassed her to the point that you drove her into a Psychiatric ward after you were locked up for testifying against you, is this true?"

"Yes it's true. I knew I was guilty of killing your mother, but not the way they said I did it. Susan was trying to make it sound premeditated and that wasn't true. Saying that I planned the murder could have gotten me life without parole or the death sentence. I took the knife over to scare her not to kill her."

"It sounds like you didn't want to do the time for such a horrific crime."

"When I first got locked up Kennedy, all I cared about was me and my well-being. Even before your mother and I got the divorce, I just couldn't do right. I knew I only wanted her, but I still wanted to have my cake and eat it too. I expected her to be there when I got done playing games."

I respected his honesty and we grew closer.

"Have you accepted Jesus as your Lord and savior and repented?"

"Yes I have baby. Who do you think help me out of the penitentiary?"

"Amen," I rejoiced.

As our relationship blossomed I talked him about my issues. How I was in and out of relationships and even my latest relationship with Sean. His insight gave me the strength to walk away from Sean.

In my car after the last break up I prayed sincerely. *God, I need you, I can't make it without you, please forgive my sins*. I was detailed about every sin. Then I asked God for the second best thing besides salvation. I asked God to give me a Godly husband.

12

I prayed for Mr. Right on a Friday and God showed him to me Monday, which was Memorial Day. Of course Rachel wanted all the details.

"Wow, girl can you teach me how to pray! That was a quick answer. How did you meet each other?"

"I wanted a funnel cake from the Hawaii State Fair. I called my girlfriend Kelly and asked her to come with me. As soon as we walked in I noticed him. He was a third-wheel with a couple. *Boy can I spot a third-wheel since I always was.*

As he turned around and smiled at Kelly, I noticed his beautiful smile. Kelly walked over and hugged him. I walked away nervous. Kelly caught up with me. She asked why I walked away.

"Who was that?" I asked.

"Oh, that was William, why?" She smiled at me.

Still smiling she said, "Why? You wanna know'em."

I paused.

"I'm gonna hook you up, I'm going back over there," Kelly said.

Kelly hated Sean. She was always trying to **hook me up** and I didn't wanna be **hooked up**. I was fet-up with these so called men. *These only good for one thing, don't even know how to hold the door open, be a gentleman, men. Oh, no I was done with that foolishness in my life.* I asked God this time; I waited on Mr. Right. Kelly excited for me asked was he dating someone, he said no. Later finding out that God told him I was his wife before we went on our first date. He was the man of God I prayed for.

I had no clue he was going to be my husband. Our first date we went parasailing, but he was a minute late picking me up. Just looking for a reason to kick'em to the curb, it was my first red flag. No dinner date trying to be romantic too soon was appealing to me, so he had a green flag as well. *Ah hah! I'm on to him now.* On the drive to the pier, he was playing Christian rap. Thinking to myself, "Now this is pretty low; using Jesus to convince me he's a good guy. *Red flag number two."* How could he use Jesus for his own benefit? One more and he is outta here. That was until the drive home he busts my bubble and put in CD number two…another Christian CD? Ok, so let me ask him.

"William, can I look through your CD collection?"

"Sure," he said.

We talked. Sure enough he went to Word of Life. I should-of known, that church could change the devil himself. He told me that's where he received salvation. I told him I'd been visiting the church and was planning to join. I shared with him, that I accepted the Lord at 15. I had no idea what came with salvation other than I wouldn't burn in hell. I didn't know I needed to read my word in order to grow and see a change in my life.

As I continued looking through William's CD collection I found some guy named Lecrae, another by the name of Flame and Trip Lee. I was wrong about him; he wasn't using Jesus for his own benefit. Assumptions can really make a fool out of people.

13

"How long did you date before marriage?" Rachel asked.

"We were married within six months."

"What did he think about your parents?"

"He had compassion towards me and our family. Just the year before we met he lost his brother. He was murdered also."

"Wow, I'm sorry to hear that Kennedy."

"Yeah, he misses him. Through Christ he was able to remain strong."

"Both of you have strong faith."

"God is all we have. First Peter chapter one will tell you test and trials will come to test your faith, but the reward is at the end, so we have to keep it moving in Christ."

Rachel starts to laugh.

"What's so funny?" I asked.

"It feels like you're the big cousin."

Rachel is an Ohio State graduate with a master in psychology, stands only 4 feet 10 inches, which is really funny since Uncle Wayne is 6'1 and her mom who was never married to Uncle Wayne is about 5'6. Short and skinny with shoulder length, jet black hair at 39 years old, she looks 25 with no kids.

"I can't believe I'm 39 and never been married. So how's married life?"

I laugh thinking; she sure looks like the younger cousin, hoping I look that good at 39. I have a 50/50 chance and it doesn't seem as if I'm taking after the Thomas family since most are tall and skinny. In my twenties my hips have spread and everyone says I'm shaped just like my momma.

"Marriage continues to be a blessing to me. I've had the privilege to marry a man after God's own heart. He's not perfect by far, especially during our dating days. I didn't know if he was righteous or *right-ish*. Even though I prayed to God for a good man, I didn't believe he existed. And if he did exist why would God bless me with him? I was an ex-fornicator, dated and slept with other women's husbands."

"Did they hit on you or did you use to hit on them?"

"No, I didn't hit on men. In my mind I wasn't a bad person. Actually, I never looked for married men or any man. The one's that I was with mentored or befriended me. I didn't like meeting knew people. In my case everyone I knew worked with me or knew someone I knew. I saw myself better than women who slept with everyone they thought was attractive, or if the man showed them a little interest. Naïve to the fullest, I wore my feelings on my shoulder. I found my heart broken in every relationship."

"Kennedy, are you serious?"

"About what?" I asked.

"You mean to tell me you thought you were better than some other women even though you were sleeping around with other women's husband."

"Yes I'm dead serious. I was a true hypocrite. Why does that seem to be so hard to believe? People do it all the time with smaller things: judge, criticize, or get irritated with someone for the very thing they do themselves. *I was blind Rachel*. Because my situation was more of a relationship and not a one night stand; telling myself you can't help who you fall in love with. Calling lust love is all deception. Not knowing that we were *all* headed for a true reality called hell. Don't get me wrong I knew it wasn't all right, but there was no conviction from the Holy Spirit that if I continued I'm going to die. Since I was military my only conviction was getting caught and having my pay cut in half."

"Wow," Rachel said in amazement.

"I was a slave to my sin stuck in deception." "So when I asked God for a man that loved Him; it was the second best thing I ever asked for."

"What was the best thing you asked for?"

"Salvation."

"Well I should have known that."

"They both saved my life. God's word says, "But if they cannot have self-control, let them marry for it is better to marry than to burn with passion," 1 Corinthians 7:9. Sometimes people are the only Jesus we see. The God on the inside of him inspired me to seek more of this God that I thought I already knew. This didn't come easy we went through the fire.

During our dating days William fell in sin.

"Really, what happened?"

"Well we were both military while dating, but I had plans to get out within a few months to further my education in nursing school. It was the end of June and he wanted to go home for the 4th of July. I had no leave days to spare. I didn't think anything about an ex-girlfriend or question him about one because I completely trusted him. After all, when we met he was celibate. It was nice, but out of my comfort zone. In previous relationships the lust was the love. When he went out of town I didn't get in contact with Sean. My mind was made up on moving forward."

"About three weeks later after William made it back to the island; the fairy tale love story hit a major bump in the road."

My phone rang.

"Hello."

"Hi pretty lady."

That's what he still calls me until this day.

"*Oh, hi William*. How are you?"

I was always excited to hear his voice, he always made me smile.

"I'm o.k.; I have something I need to tell you."

"Are you sure you ok? You sound like something is bothering you."

"Well that's why I'm calling. I have something I need to tell you. I've put it off too long as it is and I didn't know how to tell you."

"Ok William just say it. You are scaring me. Are you married or something?"

"No, I'm not married. You know when I went home to Alabama."

"Ah yeah, I dropped you off at the airport."

"Well while I was there I seen my ex-girlfriend and we."

"You what?"

There was a pause for a minute which seemed like five.

"I cheated."

In shock, this joker must be kidding me. The only Jesus I knew let me down.

"Ok...WHAT?"

"Kennedy wait, I know you aren't going to believe me but I didn't go down there to cheat on you. We were talking on the phone before I met you and I told her before we met that we could hang out.

After I met you I planned to tell her that I met you. Instead it turned into her forcing herself on me."

"Oh well I can see that, it turned into you having sex. You knew what you were going to do. TELL ME EXACTLY WHAT HAPPEN; I WANT TO KNOW EVERYTHING."

I wanted all the details, incase his story ever changed.

"I went over her house, to hang out like I told her and I planned on telling her about us. When I got there she started kissing on me and I told her that I didn't want to have sex. She kept kissing me and got my pants down to do you know what's next. I stopped her because I realized how much I wanted to be with you.

She said, "come on let's do it one more time." I told her no and I left."

Trying to catch him in I lie I said, "So you mean to tell me, when we met you were celibate, but she said let's do it one last time."

"Kennedy I knew her since high school. My past is not squeaky clean, but that's not who I am today."

Oh I took it all the way back. I threw Jesus out the window as mad as I was.

"Oh I know you not trying to get an attitude with me and you the lying cheater and you call yo-self a Christian, please spare me."

"You're right, I'm disappointed in myself and I never meant to hurt you Kennedy. I'm sorry for the hurt I've caused you, but I had to tell you the truth."

"Dude you waited a whole month to tell me the truth. Your conscious must be killing you or something."

"I have asked God for forgiveness, but I had to tell you the truth. I understand if you don't want to talk to me anymore, but I had to get that off my chest."

"You right! I don't wanna talk to your lying tail no more."

I slammed the phone down.

"God, I cried out. How could he do this to me? I'm a good person. Why do bad things happen to me?

God didn't say anything.

"Where are you God? I NEED YOU."

Sitting there in quietness, I reflected back over past relationships and how worse they were from fighting to cussing each other out to you name it, except for drugs. Oh yeah, I was too good for that. In my mind that was a sinner. I had to tell Kelly how he messed over me since she **hooked me up** and she loved me so much she wanted her husband to beat him up for me. I wouldn't let her. I knew I was no better than he was and no one had beaten me up for sleeping with the wrong man. I wanted to give him a chance because of his honesty. Something I'd never been able to do was tell the truth about my faults. I didn't want to bear the shame from all my hidden secrets. But yet this man told the truth. I would-of never known the truth if he had not told me and our whole life could-of been a lie. I think I will give him a chance.

14

A month later, I called William back.

I knew his mandatory pre-deployment training was over. Man time was flying. It was September and in November for a whole year, he would deploy. I never dated an Army man. I wasn't use to the 12 month deployments.

As I stared at the phone hoping it would ring and it would be him on the other end; I didn't want to call him. It never rang. So I finally called him.

He answers, "Hello."

Shocked, because I really wanted his answer machine, so I could say something nice-nasty and straight to the point. I wanted to forgive and be mad all at the same time.

"I forgive you."

"Really, I've been thinking about you, but didn't wanna bother you."

"Uh huh."

"I was wondering if we could try again."

Perfect, because this was the most I was saying. I did the calling what else did he want from me.

I pause. Letting him know, I'm seriously considering saying no.

"I guess we can try only one more time, but if you ever cheat again, there will be no more chances."

"Don't worry, I know what I want now."

"Ok. We will see."

We both had our minds made up after the phone call. His was to win my heart and keep it that way. My mind was determined to figure out the truth about the situation and to see if he had lied about anything else. It was time for war.

I remember every word he told me a month ago and I was going to make sure the story didn't change.

William bought me flowers and balloons on days that weren't a special occasion like Valentine's Day. My heart wasn't ready to receive.

"So what's her name?"

"What's whose name?"

"You know, your ex?"

"Is this going to make you feel better if I tell you her name?"

"Yes. I just need to know."

"Okay, but are we going to be able to move forward?"

"This is part of my healing process."

"Her name is Octavia."

It was the weirdest name I'd ever heard; I was sure no one else had that name. It was time to do some research on this girl.

This was when MySpace was cool before everyone decided to switch to Facebook. Which I never understood because I thought MySpace was way-better since you could play music. I started my research on this Octavia. Sure enough she was the only one in our age group with this ridiculous name.

Wow her page was open!

15

I need my hair to look perfect for these MySpace photos. I love Hawaii. How can you have a bad day in paradise? I love the everyday 80 degree weather with a light breeze that won't mess your hair up every time you step outside.

It's the weekend. William is still trying to make-up. I'm gonna tell'em to take me to the beach to swim with the dolphins. Then I can show off my bikini and let Octavia know…he does not miss you boo.

My phone rings. "Hello."

"Do you have plans today?" William asked politely.

"Um not yet," I said, telling a lie.

I had the whole day planned and my camera charged to catch every moment.

"Is there anything you want to do today?"

"Well I haven't got a chance to swim with the dolphins yet?"

"Well, that's not a problem sweet-thing, I got you," William said.

"Really," as if I was shocked.

"That's not a problem; I will go to the MWR and grab some tickets."

"Okay I will be ready when you get here."

My swim suit lying across the bed with the tags still on from Victoria Secret, oh yeah, I couldn't be looking all common with my Wal-Mart swim suit; it was time to step my game up. The swim suit was all white to stand out on my brown skin; I had the push up halter top that tied at the neck for my maximum cleavage I was going for, with my extra-large, low-rise bottoms on and for color I put on my floral purple and green wedges. Now these dolphins bet-not mess my hair up, splashing all over the place. I had my Mary-Kay make-up on like we were going to the military ball. Let's not forget my swim suit throw, looking like I was born and raised in Hawaii.

My door bell rings.

I know its William. I will make him wait a few minutes. Standing in the mirror making sure not one strand of hair is out of place, I hear my cell. Now he knows I don't play-that; *don't be rushing me.*

I pick up, "I'm walking out now," I said, in a polite tone of voice.

"I've been standing outside."

I open the front door without hanging up the phone; stopped his whining about the wait. His mouth fell open and his eyes lit-up.

"PRETTY-LADY, HOW-ARE-YOU?   You look beautiful.

"I'm doing great, thank you."

I was far from great on the inside. I had this raging war going on about this Octavia. Octavia's MySpace page was open and she looked a-hot-mess. Every picture she wore tights, I mean this girl had every color. I thought for sure they stop making gold tights in the 80's. Can anybody tell me, where she got those black pleather tights from? Every pose was so demeaning. I can't believe William would go from class to a-hot-mess. Every picture her backside is facing the camera with her head looking over her shoulder down toward her behind. Is there any other asset to you besides your behind?

William opened the car door for me to get in. He's always been a gentleman towards me.

"Thank you," I said with a smile.

"My pleasure."

Spending time with William was refreshing; we know we can have some fun together. Of course I was afraid of dolphins, but so what; the pictures came out great. I took my heels off since William is only 5'7, but the water looked great on his brown skinned for the photos. We never have a problem with photos. His big round brown eyes with long eye lashes that anyone woman wouldn't mind having and that smile, brings warmth to my heart.

Afterwards we grabbed a bite to eat; I could barely eat. A professional couldn't do a better job on these photos; if I could just get home to upload them. Uhh…where is the waiter with my food?

At the dinner table William slid a black ring box across the table. My eyes lit up with surprise. Everything was going through my head at once.

Thinking to myself, if I say no, he may never ask me again, but are we ready to move forward.

"Kennedy, before you say anything, let me. I knew you were my wife before our first date, after Kelly gave me your phone number and we talked for the first time. I told God that I was no longer looking for a wife, but that I would allow his will to be done. When we hung up that evening God spoke to my heart very clearly and said, "That's your wife."

"Of course I always knew in the back of my mind you would be *SOMEDAY*. In my mind we would date for a couple of years to prepare to join our lives together, but I know now is the time. There is a time and place for everything and this is our time. I love you and I want to spend the rest of my life showing you my love. Kennedy, I know it won't be easy, but I am willing. Will you marry me?"

16

He was right. Our first year was far from easy. William and I married November 1, in Hawaii. I always wanted to marry on the beach, on a hot summer day. Well, I didn't get summer, but it sure felt like it. With only a month away our families had no time to plan a trip to Hawaii. We decided to visit our families and introduce each other.

Soon as we landed in Alabama, William's mom Gloria, Granny and Papa were at the airport; both parked in loading only zone to pick us up.

William walked me to my car.

"Hey Papa, hey Granny, this is my fiancé William."

My grandmother was excepting of William right away. William leaned in to hug Papa, but Papa wouldn't hug him back. Oh here we go with the family drama. William tries to load my bags in the trunk of the car, but Papa snatches them from him.

"Granny I'll be right back; he's going to introduce me to his mom."

"Well hurry up, if I get a ticket you paying for it," she said.

"Yes ma'am."

"Hey momma," William said in this young boy tone of voice while hugging her.

Oh great don't tell me he's a momma's boy. With one arm around Gloria's shoulder William says, "Mom let me introduce you to the love of my life. Mom this is Kennedy, Kennedy this is my mother."

"Hello Kennedy," Gloria said.

"Hi, it's nice to meet you ma'am."

"Uh huh, yeah you too. We're having a barbeque at my house at 3'oclock for you and my son; bring your family so we can get to know each other," she said in a bossy tone of voice.

Gloria stood about 5'5, dark skinned, full figured, her hair was cut short, but suiting for her middle age, grey and black in color, but looks platinum. I could feel tension, but I didn't care.

"Ok yes ma'am, see you at 3'oclock."

The only family I had besides my great grandmother, papa's mom and her sister my great aunt was my grandparents and my Aunt Mia. Auntie Mia is Granny's oldest daughter my mother's big sis. She moved down my freshman year of high school. I asked Auntie Mia to come to the barbeque along with Papa and Granny in case I needed back up. We made it to the barbeque late. Papa thought he knew where he was going. When we pulled up, their house had life to it. Kids were running around, I could hear his family laughing and talking from the back yard.

Frightened, I was a learned loaner. Growing up without my sibling and being around kids was all new to me and his nieces and nephews asked a lot of questions. I didn't know how to communicate with children, so they stared at me and I stared at them. Hi was as far as I could go out of my comfort zone.

Walking into their home I said, "Hi Ms. Gloria these are my grandparents James and Roslyn."

"Hello, I'm Gloria the groom's mother, y'all come on in. Go on and fix ya'selves a plate. We already started eating."

I thought for sure she told me the cook out was for me and William. You think they would-of waited until we got there to start eating. We were only 15 minutes late and by that time his family ate, working on seconds and started playing cards. Oh no, how rude. Thinking to myself this is where rude meets rude. My grandparents have lost all their social skills from their youth due to television. *Lord help me*. They're not talking-and why did they turn the TV on in the den? Yes, Papa found his way in front of my future in-laws TV. That's why I brought my back up, Aunt Mia. Auntie Mia and Granny joined me in Gloria's dining room.

Granny said, "How they-gone eat without us? I thought the party was for you and William?"

"I know granny. It's okay."

"And this food is bland."

"Granny it's okay. Do you want some salt and pepper?"

"No."

Gloria and William came in from outside after we finished our food. William sits and Gloria stood next to my chair.

"How's the food?" Gloria asked.

"MMM...it was great, thank you." I said.

While hoping Granny doesn't embarrass me, Gloria speaks her mind.

"I know they grown, BUT IM NOT READY FOR MY SON TO GET MARRIED."

Granny looked up at her like, oh no she didn't.

"Well that's just too bad," Granny said.

"I know, but that's my baby."

"He aint no baby, that's a grown man."

I didn't stop Granny right away, because I really wanted her to put Gloria in her place so I wouldn't have to.

"Well Ms. Gloria, if William and I pay for your plane ticket would you like to come to the wedding?"

"I'm gonna see my baby get married, but his grandma need a ticket too. Then I know his sister gone-be-hot, if she can't come. I can't come by myself."

Is this lady crazy? We can't pay for all these folks.

"Why don't y'all get married here?" Gloria insisted.

What? Now I know she has really lost it. Who would pick Alabama over Hawaii to get married?

"What's the big rush anyway? Are y'all pregnant or something?"

"Are you kidding me?" Granny stated madly.

"No we're not pregnant and we're getting married in Hawaii. We offered to pay YOUR plane ticket." I was starting to get ugly.

William hasn't opened his mouth.

Granny ended the dinner, "Thank you for the food Gloria, but we're leaving now; let's go Kennedy, and go get your Papa. We don't have to listen to this mess."

17

The family issues affected us greatly, but no matter how jacked up our families were, we loved them.

"Are you going to let your mother talk to me like that when I'm your wife?"

"No. I'm sorry Kennedy; I wasn't expecting her to act like that. Honestly, I wasn't prepared for any of that."

"What are you going to do when the unexpected comes up? You can't let people belittle me; you're supposed to protect me."

"Baby I did talk to my mother after the fact."

"But you allowed me to be humiliated."

"I'm sorry baby. Please forgive me. I put you second in my life."

"And who is first?"

"Of course, God honey."

"I had to make sure."

"So do you forgive me?" William questioned me.

I smiled and said, "Yes I forgive you. I really didn't know what to do in that situation either."

"See I knew it. That's something we will have to pray about."

We had a small intimate wedding November 1 with only our close friends. We didn't allow anyone to ruin our sacred union.

William deployed with the Army 9 days after our wedding. During this time William's ex-girlfriends were still trying to contact him and Gloria got worse. Four months after the wedding Gloria writes me this long letter. I'm in the states not on deployment, pick up the phone lady. In the letter she tells me how selfish I am for having the wedding in Hawaii. How she missed her only son's wedding. I have tried to be nice to this lady. I understand she lost her son the year before William and I wedded, but by the end of this 8 page letter of blessing me out, avoiding her was out the window.

I called her.

"Hi Gloria, I just read your letter and I'm really disappointed."

She starts yelling, "I HAVE THE RIGHT TO SAY MY OPINION IF I WANT TO."

She was so mad, she hung up on me. I had no choice, but to tell William when he called. By this time I have no tolerance for William as if he wrote the letter himself. I checked his email that day and his ex who use to work with him sent him the movie Made of Honor. Of all movies this was the utmost disrespect. Why? Because the wedding ends up getting called off because of another person. He responds back with a thank you!

I start shouting in our two bedroom apartment, "I'M SICK OF THIS. I-HAVE-HAD-IT!"

When William called, my mouth must-of been moving 90 miles per hour and I didn't let off the gas either.

"You and my mother better learn to get along or not talk at all for now, because I can't keep going through this while I'm over here."

"You can't keep going through what? You aint going through nothing, I'm the one dealing with all your baggage. Don't forget what you did to me, all these exes popping up and yo-nagging momma make me want to scream."

"Hello, HELLO! Oh I know he didn't hang up on me."

My phone rang.

"HELLO."

"I'm sorry, I shouldn't-of hung up. Don't forget she maybe a lot of things, but she still my momma."

"You know what William, I can't do this momma's boy stuff, she don't cook and wash yo-dirty draws...I do."

"I want to be there for you, I really do, but right now I can't fix yawl's problems from here. I'm at war, seems like in every aspect of my life right now.

18

I'm sick and tired of being sick and tired. This is too hard. I knew who I could talk to. Sean worked with me. Maybe I'll call and talk to him. No I'm not calling him. He couldn't get it right. Why call him.

I'm going to fix William. If he don't care about this marriage neither do I. Immediately a thought came to me; just leave him, you don't have to put up with this. No I'm not going to leave, but I want him to know how I feel. I was angry. But in this very moment without notice, I made a deal with the devil.

After I'd cooled down a few days later, I still had thoughts about making William feel as low as I did. I didn't cast my thoughts down to make them obedient to Christ, 2 Corinthians 10:5.

I heard the enemy say just call Sean. While out at the mall I remember wanting to walk into him or see him out somewhere.

I'd just bought a 52" TV still in the box. I think I will stop buy Best Buy and pick up a TV stand. Well the TV stand came up to 300 dollars, which I paid cash for along with the TV, but I was too cheap to pay 100 dollars for the service department to deliver and set the stand up for me.

Well who can I call? Kelly and her husband are out of town. Let me call Mya and see what she's up to today.

The phone rings. Mya answers, "Hello."

"What's up sis?"

Were like sisters Mya's husband Darren and William are best friends.

"Nothing much."

"Did you talk to my brother today?" I questioned.

"No I haven't talked to him yet."

"If you talk to Darren before I talk to William, tell him to have William call me. We been arguing again over his momma and these females."

"KENNEDY, now you need to leave Will alone. They are at war and it's not a game over there in Iraq. Now if something happen to him you wouldn't know what to do. You act like he over there with a female. You talking about women on the other side of the world from your husband."

"Yeah I know you right. But it seems like he don't protect me. How's my God baby doing? Tell him TT misses him."

"Girl D.J. is being bad and eating everything."

"Well you make sure you feed my baby. I feel bad for Darren with D.J. being yawls first baby and him having to leave just 12 days later."

Mya laughed at me being silly. "Yeah he misses him. I'm just ready for this deployment to be over Kennedy."

"That's why we gotta stay busy. Girl I bought this TV stand for that TV and I refused to pay Best Buy a 100 dollar installation fee."

"Girl I told you about being cheap, what you want me to do; I don't know how to put it together."

"Come on we can try."

"No Kennedy, when me and Darren put D.J.'s dresser together it ended up being lopsided...NO."

"Well what am I supposed to do than Mya, leave it in the box? You know people breaking in these apartments over here. If the thieves look in the window and see my TV in the box, they gonna wait for me to go to work and we gone be next, all over a TV stand."

"No means no Kennedy."

"Alright then, I gotta try to find someone to put this TV stand together for less than 100 dollars. I'll call you when I get my house in order."

"Bye silly," Mya said.

"Bye."

"Call Sean," Satan said.

The enemy waited patiently for me to get off the phone. You don't have anyone else to call he said. By the way, don't forget how William talked to you the other day, you still owe him.

I picked up the phone and dialed his number. "Hello," he answered on the second ring.

"Are you busy?" I asked.

I started hoping he would say yes, so I could say ok sorry to bother you and hang up.

Of course he said, "No, not at all."

"Well I actually needed some help."

"Help with what?"

"I bought this TV stand and refused to pay the 100 dollar installation fee and I need some help putting it together."

"Ok I'm free now."

Thinking to myself, that's great since its morning; I have all day before the sun goes down. Nothing could happen in broad daylight.

"That's great. Ok. See you soon."

19

The doorbell rings.

"Hi, come in. First off, thank you for your help."

"Oh you welcome."

I already took the stand out the box so he could get right to it. He walked into the living room where the stand was lying on the floor, and picked up the box to get a visual.

"Okay let's do it."

"Excuse me, do what?"

"Oh I'm going to need your help."

This plan was not thought out properly. I just wanted him to come over so I can through it up in William's face if he ticked me off again. Why does he need my help? So what the stand has three levels. He needs to be a man.

"You do."

"Ah yeah. That's probably why they wanted to charge so much. This aint no K-Mart stand. This will take at least an hour and a half to put together."

"It will."

He laughed, "Do you have somewhere to go?"

"No."

While he's putting the stand together he decides he wants to reminisce.

"I was stupid to let you go Kennedy. I thought we were going to be together, because you always forgave me.

Satan returned "see he loves you. You don't have to beg William.

I could feel the anger rise up in me towards William all at the same time.

"Kennedy I lust for you."

What? Lust, lust is not love; even an unbeliever knows the difference. But the anger and the revenge to get back at William was stronger now. I don't care about the ex and his lust, but the anger from the hurt that William has put me through is greater.

Sean kissed me on my neck and I haven't been kissed in a while, now I'm burning with lust. I'm only going to do what William said happened between him and the girl with the weird name.

In the heat of the moment, I felt dirty; I started to feel love not anger towards my husband. Where did the voice go? I guess he ran out of ideas.

I jumped up pushing him off of my body.

"Kennedy what's wrong?"

"Everything is wrong; I'm cheating on my husband for starters, GET OUT MY HOUSE."

"Baby it's okay."

"I'm not your baby and I'm going to tell my husband about this."

"What? He's going to leave you."

I wasn't his baby then. I wanted him to know he couldn't hang nothing over my head.

He laughed at me.

"I'm serious. Get out my house."

20

The front door was next to the kitchen as he left out of my house and out of my life. I closed the door and went to my room and cried loudly. My heart was in pain.

In all my sexual experiences outside of marriage, I'd never felt dirty. Even when I slept with someone's husband I didn't feel dirty, I knew it wasn't right but it didn't feel wrong.

This time I felt convicted in my spirit. I knew I was going to die if I didn't change my life. Immediately I repented of my sins.

"God I messed up, I don't know what I'm gonna do. God please forgive me, help me Lord I need you."

Letting go of the pillow soaked in tears, I got in the shower.

"It's Sunday. I'm going to the 6'oclock service, I need you God."

In the car headed to church, I asked the Lord, "How can I tell William this?"

I didn't get an answer from God. At least not right away. I called Mya to find out where she was parking since we attended the same church.

Walking towards the church together Mya ask me, "Are you okay?"

"What? Oh girl yeah. Why you ask? Do I look like something's wrong?"

Lying on the way in church, maybe the Lord will change me on the way out.

"Well yeah you aint said a word and I know that's not like you."

"Girl I'm just ready to receive this word."

"Uh huh, well whenever you feel like telling me, I'll be here."

The music is playing and the atmosphere is heavenly. Lord I don't feel worthy to be here in your presence.

At the end of service the pastor asked if anyone needed to rededicate their life or join the church, neither one of us were members. I knew God was calling me to put him first in my life and to rededicate my life.

So immediately I asked Mya, "Do you want to join the church?"

At least she won't think something if I ask her about joining. Now this is a big church so we are both nervous about walking to the front.

"Umm no I'm ok," Mya said.

I could see that she wanted to; her knees were shaking.

"Well I'm going up," I said.

"Okay. I'll go too."

I rededicated my life back to Christ.

21

The next day, Tracy my high school friend called. We always kept in touch.

"Hey Kennedy."

"Hey girl."

"Look I know I've been saying I'm coming to visit you. I put in for vacation for next week and it was approved. Can I come next week?"

"Of course you can come, but I won't be on leave. I don't have any days to take. I'd hate for you to come out here and have to sit in the house while I'm at work."

"It's fine. We can hang out when you get off, but first I need to say this. I know you have changed, so I wouldn't ask you to take me to the club. I know that's not you anymore."

Wow that was a huge relief.

"Ok yeah, because I'm trying to live my life the way God has called me to live, but there are plenty of things to do besides club. Anyways I would like you to meet my friend Mya when you come out. I know yawl will click."

"Ok sounds like fun."

Lining up things to do like snorkeling, jet skiing, and parasailing and if we have time, swim with the dolphins. Of course, I can take her to a luau, and rent scooters to cruise the island.

Tracy flew into Honolulu Friday, day before the 4th of July. Mya and I had plans to barbeque on the beach and watch the fireworks.

Driving into the airport, I see Tracy standing on the curb with her hair dyed a honey blonde, in spiral curls that reached her shoulders which looked really nice on her brown skin complexion, in jean shorts and a black tank top with flip flops and oversized sun glasses with her Louis Vuitton hand bag resting on her luggage. *How could I miss her?*

After popping the trunk to my car, I jumped out.

"TRACY!"

"KENNEDY!"

"I'm so glad you're here."

"I know me too, and the view was beautiful while landing. I could feel the heat while waiting for the flight attendants to open the door. I'm hot now."

"That's Hawaii for you. Get in, the airs on."

"Are you tired?" I asked.

"Not really, I slept the whole way. I know you probably don't drink, but I bought me some vodka and it knocked me out."

She was right. Drinking was never a stronghold and easy to let go of.

"No I don't drink anymore. This evening we can go to this restaurant; it's great, the food is delicious, five star service and it revolves so we can see the whole city of Waikiki."

Tracy was familiar with the restaurant. She said, "Okay, I believe they have a restaurant like that in Atlanta. One of those rappers own it, I believe."

"Tomorrow I will introduce you to Mya; her husband is deployed with William."

"I think it's great Kennedy, you and your husband are into the church. I mean I believe, but I'm not where you are."

Thinking to myself, where am I? God I can't talk to her about my life, she won't understand.

"Tracy I'm not a perfect person."

That was far as I could go with my testimony.

"I know that, but you have come a long way. The Kennedy I knew would fight at the drop of a dime. The way you look at life is totally different."

"It's not me its God and even still I mess up, but I thank God for his undeserving grace."

"Amen, Tracy said."

We enjoyed ourselves at the restaurant.

The next morning was 4th of July.

"Are you ready to barbeque on the beach?"

I could tell from her facial expressions the things I liked doing were starting to bore her. Out of respect for my lifestyle she didn't ask me to party since she already told me she wouldn't.

"Sure." Nonchalantly Tracy said.

Tracy and Mya clicked just as I thought they would. Mya's heart was ready to surrender to God and be the wife and mother she had been called to be.

The night on the beach was cut short by rain. Worry is starting to set in. I wish I didn't have to work while Tracy is here. How can I show her a good time?

On Sunday I asked, "Tracy did you bring church clothes?"

Standing over her while she was pulling out her outfit for the day, I noticed clubbing clothes.

"No. Are we going to church?"

"Yes this evening, but that's okay because those jeans and one of my button-up shirts will do for church."

"*Really?*"

"Really, and those flip flops are okay too. We can go snorkeling before since I have to work tomorrow."

"What time is the second service?"

"Oh we're going to the fourth service and it's at 6pm."

"Y'all have church at night over here, wow that's really nice. I would be able to go to church every Sunday, if they did that on the mainland."

"I know it is. There's really no excuse for me missing church."

"I forgot to tell you, I can't swim."

Oh no. How am I going to show her a good time when all the activities I have planned are water events? Tracy enjoyed the view of the ocean, since she was afraid of water and the rest of the week's forecast was rain. The Friday before she left I decided to rent a room downtown Waikiki and invite Mya and we could hang out without having to drive 30 minutes home. We could site see and have clean fun. We called Mya that evening and we waited until about 10:30 p.m. for her to show. By this time we had eaten, walked around and made it back to the room. In the room was two queen size beds. I'm lying sideways face down on the one next to the windows with my feet hanging off the bed, half sleep. While Tracy is patiently waiting for Mya to show up, I heard the Lord tell me not to leave the room. If so, someone is going to get hurt.

Right after, Mya knocks on the door.

I try to play sleep even though I was exhausted from the whole week of working and trying to entertain. Mya comes in telling Tracy about this club downtown they could go to. I'm really not trying to leave the room now.

Satan returns saying, "Tracy hasn't done anything since she's been here, you should show her a good time."

But I know for sure God told me not to leave the room.

Mya and Tracy both saying at the same time, "*Kennedy wake up lets go out.*"

"No I'm sleepy, y'all waited too late."

Tracy couldn't stand it anymore, "Come on Kennedy this is my last night here and we haven't done much."

"Y'all go without me."

Guilt set in. I remembered the Lord saying someone is going to get hurt. I can't let anything happen to Tracy on my watch.

"Come on Kennedy," they insisted.

"Ok."

On the way out the room I prayed to God. Lord, please don't let any of us get hurt, but I learned God's word is final.

22

It was 4 a.m. when we left the club. Believing that the Lord answered my prayer because we didn't get into a fight, no one went to jail, or committed adultery and we were all in one piece. Walking back to the car in the parking deck, Mya is walking a couple steps in front of me and Tracy; seemed like out of the blue this guy and his friend approaches her. I'm leery because I remember the word God gave me. Someone is going to get hurt.

Parked next to Mya's Jaguar is the same guy's Range Rover. This doesn't seem to be a stranger. As we start backing out the parking spot he motions for Mya to roll down her window and ask if he could treat us all to breakfast. Mya answered for all of us and said yes.

I'm blowing my breath saying, *"we don't know them; this is not a good idea."*

Tracy said, "It will be okay, free breakfast and he's cute."

"You the only one single up in here, it won't be okay. Mya I know you done lost your mind."

At the restaurant Kevin and Chris is what they told us their names were. Chris was the one that invited us; the one Tracy thought was cute. I didn't trust him. Kevin was single with a baby on the way. Chris told us he was divorced with a child. He showed interest in Mya even though she had her wedding ring on which really made me want to throw-up with all that I'd been through. After breakfast he gave Tracy his phone number in case she wanted to talk and he asked for both Mya's and Tracy's Myspace name just to chat. Tracy told him that she was leaving that evening, but it didn't seem to bother him at all. He didn't ask me nothing during the whole conversation. I put MY-HUSBAND in everything I had to say to either of them.

By the time we got back to the room it was 5:30a.m.

I thanked the Lord for his protection and asked him for His forgiveness as I showered and laid down. William called at 6:00a.m. after our free breakfast, I told him right away. I had to release it and wasn't sure how I was going to release the fact that I wasn't faithful right before all of this. He was *hot* that we were out with strangers and the free meal was fuel to the fire. He had every right to be. It was disrespectful. I'm not going to be able to tell him about the other thing; I will just take this to my grave.

23

A week later while cleaning my apartment, God spoke again, "Mya is cheating on her husband with Chris."

I reasoned with myself saying that can't be right. They didn't exchange phone numbers, him and Tracy did. It was on me to talk to Mya, but then I would have to share my story and I already made up in my mind that I was taking that to the grave.

A month past, Mya and I got connected and started attending bible study called life group. The same month, William came home from deployment for R and R. My life group leader told me, Kennedy you're going to have a baby. I saw it in a dream.

A week after William left, Mya started fasting. It seemed like every other week she was on a fast.

"Kennedy I need God to move in my life."

"Is there something wrong? You can talk to me, you really can."

"No, there's nothing wrong."

While I was at work, Mya called me and said her right side of her body was numb.

"Go to the hospital, that's signs of a stroke."

"No I don't want to."

"If you don't; I'm going to call the ambulance for you. You can't mess around when you having signs of a stroke. Are you crazy?"

"Ok. I'll go."

On my lunch break I called to check on her.

"What did they say?"

"They said I'm pregnant. I don't know what I'm gonna do Kennedy."

It wasn't Darren's baby. God reminded me of what He said that night in the hotel room, someone is going to get hurt, and my heart felt as if it fell in my lap.

24

I told her exactly what God told me. I know it's not your
husband's baby, because the Lord told me you were sleeping
with Chris, but I didn't want to believe it.

Mya broke down into tears.

"Yes it's true and I don't know how I'm going to tell
my husband this."

"I'm not going to keep this baby Kennedy."

For once I had to stand up for what was right.

"Yes you are, don't kill your baby. Give your baby a
chance. This is a life were talking about."

"I'm going to lose my husband."

I knew how she felt. The thought of losing the one you took
for granted. I was no better than she was.

"Mya you have to tell your husband the truth."

Thinking *what am I saying, what a hypocrite.*

"I know I'm going to tell him over the phone, I feel
more comfortable doing it that way."

She told him. This lead to William and I discussing the
situation. Her courage allowed me to tell my own truth.

That same day the truth set me free and broke the shackles of shame off of me. I could stand having girded my waist with truth Eph 6:14.

25

William wanted to know the whole story. After I told him everything, he said, "I'm hurt and that's not going to go away right away, but I'm not leaving you."

"Revenge is not mine, it's the Lords. I found out the hard way about taking matters into my own hands."

"I need time to allow God to heal me," William said.

"Okay William, whatever you need."

We hung up.

"God thank you for being gracious towards me."

When William forgave me I understood God's love for His children. Though we don't deserve it, He loves us anyway. I gave my all to God and never looked back. I learned not to play with fire because you will get burned. Scriptures says in James 4:7 "Submit yourselves therefore to God. Resist the devil, and he will flee from you."

Mya gave birth to my second God baby Grace Walker, without her husband. Shame kept me in bondage and from possibly saving their marriage, but the power of truth helped me save Grace's life.

Rachel couldn't stop crying.

Rachel said, "*I had an abortion before.* I use to think about that baby all the time. You're the first person I ever told. I couldn't speak the word *abortion.*"

"Rachel, do you know where shame comes from?"

"No, where does it come from?"

"It comes from sin, but refusing to forgive yourself. See because, even though I asked God for forgiveness, I didn't forgive myself of my shameful behavior which lead to me sweeping it under the rug and being of no value to God in how He changed my life. It was one of the first things that came into the world when Adam and Eve fell. The bible says they hid themselves from God because they were naked."

"Kennedy I'm ready to give my life to Christ, I want to know him the way you know him."

"Okay, repeat this prayer after me. Father I ask that you will forgive my sins. I believe that you died on the cross for me, to save me. You did what I could not do for myself. I come to you now and ask you to take control of my life, I give it to you. Help me to live every day in a way that pleases you. I love you, Lord."

Rachel repeated the prayer.

"Guess what Rachel? All your shameful sins are underneath the blood of Jesus. He has washed you clean. William and I have stayed connected to Jesus and since God has called my husband to be a pastor, that's why he couldn't make it to my birthday party. He is being mentored by our pastor and will be ministering God's word Sunday."

"Wow, God has brought y'all a long way, huh?"

"Yes He has."

Rachel said, "I'm glad the whole family is coming since Uncle Patrick is throwing the party, but through your forgiveness I think we can all grow from this."

"Well dad has been out of prison 5 years now and our relationship is strong, though people try to shut my mouth, and try to bring up his past. I can't live my life not forgiving when Jesus forgave all my sins. I believe God's word is true, you reap what you sow. Through forgiving dad, I believe I was able to reap forgiveness from my husband."

"I never looked at it like that. How do you feel now?" Rachel asked.

"I feel free...free at last," I said with joy in my heart.

www.ingramcontent.com/pod-product-compliance
Lightning Source LLC
Chambersburg PA
CBHW071333130626
46556CB00004B/1874